THE BALLAD OF RICKY

J S SUTTON

First published in Great Britain as a softback original in 2021

All characters and events in this publication, other than those clearly in the public domain, are fictitious and any resemblance to real persons, living or dead, is purely coincidental.

Typeset in Palatino

Design, typesetting and publishing by UK Book Publishing

www.ukbookpublishing.com

ISBN: 978-1-914195-43-3

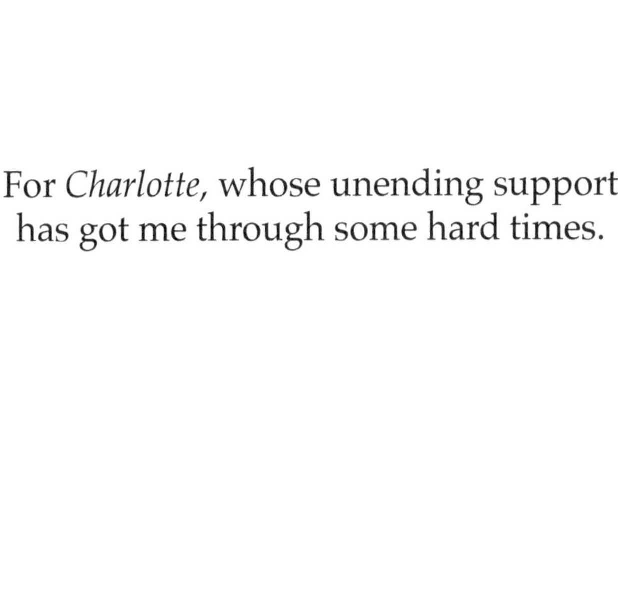

For *Charlotte,* whose unending support has got me through some hard times.

Author's Note: this book is best read while listening to *Dark Synth/Ambient Music*

PART 1:

Retribution

1

When Ricky left David's apartment on the twenty third floor of the apartment block in East New London known as Aurora Heights, he felt a slight elation at the huge amount of money in his pocket. And he knew exactly where he'd spend a chunk of it. The Neon Potato.

The Neon Potato was the place to be at times like this. If you had the big enough wad of credits you could get anything you wanted. It was New Soho after all. And anything goes in New Soho. New Chinatown too, if you knew the right people. Which he did, very well. Now that Chong Yu was on the colony, it meant there was an opening for a seat at the table. The big table. Ricky smiled at this. The possibilities open to him now he was back in normal society.

He caught the next electric bus pod down to New Soho, hiding his pistol in his long coat. He wanted a little fun. Since he got back to the city after his long stint on the colony, Ricky had only been obsessed with one thing. Killing David Wright. Not just for busting his nose and knocking out a few teeth, but for being a rat too and causing the war that he'd barely escaped from. He'd found out the same way most people on the colony did. Word of mouth from repeat offenders. Now that was out of the way, and he had a bit of money, he decided to indulge in his other passions. Getting stoned and getting laid. The bus pod stopped in New Soho and Ricky got off. He looked around to find the Neon Potato, finding it and walked inside. It was night time now and the neon lights were pulsating at him. Inside, he found a table and sat down. UV heaven. It was different than he remembered. The music throbbed with the lights and people didn't so much dance, rather moved their limbs slowly. He felt his gun in his coat, and felt a slither of satisfaction as the cold steel pushed against his ribs. A tremendous amount of safety too. No one would fuck with him, with this piece in his hand. He stroked it, lovingly and smiled. He pulled his gun out under the table and checked his bullet count situation. He had enough for what he planned on doing. 'After the fun' he thought.

Hours later, he left the Neon Potato, drunk with a hooker on his arm.

"Are you one of Alejandro's girls?" he slurred at her.

"Hasn't anybody told you?" she asked in reply, "Alejandro's dead, killed his top bitch and then himself."

"Jesus," he said.

She went down on him for half an hour behind a dumpster in a dark alleyway, then he paid her and she left. He felt somewhat empty after the news of Alejandro's death. 'That's not like him,' he thought. He'd known Alejandro since they were kids, Alejandro used to buy drugs in the slums for them to take wherever there weren't any cameras. Synthetics were his speciality. Why the hell would he kill his top bitch? Then himself for that matter? Something didn't add up. He had to find out why. He took the next electric bus pod down to the Portuguese slums just south of New Battersea.

2

When he got there, he went straight to Alejandro's caravan. The place was quiet. No lights on. There was still police tape covering the door. Ricky thought that somebody would've snapped the place up now that it's vacant. He guessed no one wanted to live in a place where a murder/suicide happened. He found a broken bottle on the floor and used it to cut through the police tape. Brushing it aside he walked in. He relied on the dim streetlight to navigate his way round the caravan. Other than that, it was pitch black. Somebody had spray painted the outlines of Alejandro and Tiffany's bodies where they fell. The blood still stained the carpet like spilled wine. Beside these, Ricky found an unlit roach, he sniffed it, Angel Dust. Alejandro used to get lit on a regular basis. So much so that he wouldn't be able to lift a gun, let alone fire it at someone. Suddenly, he heard a squawk of a police siren, so he left hastily. 'Better come back in the morning' he thought 'I'm too drunk and paranoid now.'

He found a cheap hotel not far from the slums. Dirty, smelled funny and not even cockroaches would call it home, but it was a place where he could get his head on a pillow and he was happy with that. The proprietor was a balding, heavy-set man with ill-fitting clothes and hair on his protruding beer belly. He had hair everywhere but his head it seemed.

Ricky noticed he had a spaced out look in his eye and it took him several minutes to get his attention.

"A room for the night please," he said.

"Twenty credits," the proprietor answered "room three two nine."

Ricky paid with cash and the proprietor's eyes lit up.

"Name?" he said.

"Ricky Walters," Ricky lied, it wasn't his real name. He was too embarrassed to reveal his real name to anyone.

"Ok Mr Walters," the proprietor said, "you have the presidential suite, room four eight one, top floor."

"Price?"

"Thirty two credits."

Ricky paid and got the lift to the top floor.

The presidential suite was just a small room

with a large bed, TV, counter, mini bar and a small bathroom. The sheets looked clean and Ricky assumed that these were the only ones they bothered washing on a daily basis. The thought of the cleanliness of the other rooms made him shudder in disgust. He put his gun on the counter then collapsed on the bed.

Screams arose in the darkness. Gunfire. Blood trickling through dead hands. Bisected bodies lay everywhere. She stood over him, smiling. He sat up. His brothers lay dead in the mud and dust. A cluster storm was coming.

He awoke screaming. 'Just a dream' he thought. He pushed himself up from the bed. A line of saliva followed him up and he wiped his mouth on his sleeve. The rain pattered against the window. He rubbed the sleep from his eyes and picked up his gun, holstering it inside his long coat. He decided to visit Alejandro's caravan again in the light of day, to see if he could solve the mystery of the situation.

"Nice night?" the proprietor asked, as Ricky was leaving.

"Kinda," Ricky said as he opened the lobby door.

In the slums, he walked past beggars, whores and pickpockets. 'This place needs gentrification,' he thought 'how can anyone live like this?'

He got to Alejandro's caravan in, what seemed like, no time at all.

As he entered, he heard the rain pitter patter on the tin roof. Everything was where he'd left it the night before. In his improved vision, he saw the sofas, the table and the kitchenette in the corner of the room. The phone on the table was still off the hook. It had a splatter of dried blood on the dial. Ricky picked it up, no dial tone, the service must've been cut off after a few weeks of the caravan being vacant. With care, he placed it back down on the table and continued looking around. He walked into Tiffany's room. There, he searched the draws of the bedside table and came across empty little coin bags of what looked like the remnants of Ko Sang, a drug from New Chinatown similar to heroin. He knew Tiffany was on it because he'd taken her to New Chinatown to get it, and she'd usually let him have some for the trouble of getting her there safely. He assumed the cops had taken the full bags as evidence.

He left the slums and decided to go to New Chinatown. He wanted some Ko Sang and he wanted it now. This process reminded him of the old Sherlock Holmes books he read in school. He always used it, even in the colony, he used to get it smuggled down to him via the Boss. He was amazed he didn't get some sooner, the cravings pulsed through him, it felt like standing too close to an amplifier in a club and feeling the bass drum vibrate in his chest. All he could think about, when he rejoined civilised society, was killing David and getting stoned. And laid, of course.

In New Chinatown, he went straight to the old dealer. He owned a shop on the corner near the hotel Chong Yu used to live in. He was still there. Good old Kung Fo had what he needed right now. The Ko Sang was a bit more expensive than Ricky remembered, but it was good shit.

Hours later, he was in the hotel room again, cooking the purple powder in a spoon. He extracted the produced liquid into a syringe, tapped his forearm and injected the magic stuff. When it kicked in, he fell back on the bed and his head started to swim. The syringe still sticking out his arm. He assumed the foetal position and he felt at home. Like he was back in the womb. Hands dancing along his skin.

He maintained that position til it wore off. He got up and rubbed his eyes. He was none the smarter for the experience.

"Fucking Sherlock Holmes lied to me again," he found himself saying.

He retrieved the syringe from his arm and threw it in the bin. He vowed never to use again, it felt like an empty vow because he knew in a few hours the cravings would return and he'd be desperately digging through the bin looking for his old needle.

3

Ricky decided to go back to New Soho. He wanted to rule the roost. Soon, this whole city would be his for the taking, and nobody was going to stop him. He was going to make his mark and become a living legend.

When he got there, he went straight for the Neon Potato. If he wanted to make his mark and own the city, he had to start somewhere. He went up to the bar and asked for the manager and a Purple Johnny, which was a mixture of After Shock Red and WKD Blue. The manager was a big black guy by the name of Big Tito, Ricky had encountered him before on the sewage bayou on the outskirts of New London. He was a tough son of a bitch, but only because he had his muscle grafted on and kept there by wiring connected to his brain from his shoulder. Take that wiring away, he's as weak as a kitten. Big Tito came to the bar, a look of slight recognition in his eye, but he shook his head to indicate that he was probably mistaken.

"What can I do for you, Mr…? He said.

"Walters," Ricky lied again, "I was wondering if we could have a chat in your office?"

"Ok," Big Ttio said, "follow me."

They sat down in a darkened room, lit only by UV lights which enhanced the colouring of the body paint his whores were wearing. Ricky smiled at the idea that soon they were going to be his, just like the club. Some people would sneer at the fact that technically they were going to be sloppy seconds, but Ricky had been on the colony that long he didn't mind.

"Now," Big Tito began, "how can I help you?"

Ricky unholstered his pistol and pointed it at Big Tito.

"Simple," he said, "I want the club."

Big Tito laughed and pointed a bigger gun at Ricky, a 9mm ultra-revolver, bigger than your average revolver. The whores started to giggle and Ricky found himself getting angry. Quickly, they both stood up. An old fashioned stand off. Neither of them standing down. Ricky wanted the club, Big Tito wanted to keep it. Suddenly, they both opened fire and ducked away for cover, Big Tito behind his desk, Ricky behind the office door.

"Come on white boy," Big Tito said, throwing his gun away, "let's see what you've really got."

Ricky holstered his weapon and entered the

office. They squared up and Big Tito grabbed Ricky by the neck and threw him up against the wall, squeezing tightly. Ricky began to feel dizzy as he struggled to breathe. He managed to lift his arms up and give Big Tito a few punches before he started to black out. In his near asphyxiated delirium, Ricky managed to pull the wiring from Big Tito's neck. All the strength left Big Tito's arm and he dropped Ricky on the ground. As he started to come round he withdrew his weapon again. Pointing it at Big Tito, he ordered him to sign the club, and all his assets, over to him. Which Big Tito did, hastily.

Big Tito gathered his things and left. Ricky walked out the office sometime later and, lifting his brand new 9mm ultra-revolver, smiled. He was on the first step to owning this city.

A few days later, Ricky was walking through New Chinatown. He was going to Kung Fo's for some more product. Ko Sang would help, though he swore never to use again, he thought one more hit won't hurt. He walked into the shop and was greeted by an old, decrepit looking chinese woman. Kung Fo's mother perhaps? She looked at Ricky and shook her head in what could've been disgust. Ricky wasn't sure.

"I'm here to see Kung Fo," he said.

She shook her head again and walked to the

back, shouting something in Cantonese.

Moments later, Kung Fo appeared.

"You wan' product?"

"Kung Fo," Ricky said, smiling, "you know me too well."

Kung Fo produced a small bag of the magic, purple powder.

"Three fifty," he said.

Ricky reached into his pocket and took out his wallet.

"Three fifty on the button."

"What is 'on the button'?"

"Nevermind," Ricky said, and he handed over the cash and took the Ko Sang, putting it in his pocket.

Back at the Neon Potato, Ricky lined the purple stuff and took a sniff hit. Pure Ko Sang rushed into his system as he sat back in his big chair. He felt great, on top of the world. The music outside his office vibrated through him. His whores cooked the rest and took their own, individual hits while one of them unzipped his trousers and went down on him.

"This is the life," he found himself saying.

She got up and wiped her mouth when he'd finished, smearing UV body paint, and then he took another sniff hit.

'Last one of the night,' he thought and he went

outside to get a drink. The Purple Johnny was with him in seconds, as he was the new manager he was entitled to free drinks whenever he wanted them and didn't have to wait for other customers to receive their orders, and he walked to the dancefloor. There was a particularly beautiful woman dancing, grinding almost, against one of the mirrors in the wall. Was she drunk? Or high maybe?

"Hello," he shouted over the music.

She smiled at him and said hi back.

"Haven't seen you here before," he said, "popular place for you?"

"Yeah," she said and carried on dancing.

She wore a red beret over long, blonde bangs, a turtleneck jumper in what looked like black, skinny, dark jeans and black stilettos. Her name was Maxine. 'Max' to her friends. Ricky felt an instant attraction. 'Maybe this is the one' he was thinking. But he put that thought out of his mind.

Hours later, they were together in the office. Taking sniffs of Ko Sang and fucking. Ricky had paid for her drinks all night and now he was getting rewarded. She did whatever he wanted her to do. When they were finished, she got up and left, Ricky never saw her again.

In the morning, Ricky forced himself up from the giant, purple, heart shaped, silk covered bed in his office. He was tired and aching from the night's exertions. He rubbed his eyes to clearly greet the day, stretched then got up. He asked the building's voice activated computer what time it was.

"Eleven am," it replied, as lifeless as any computer would be.

Half the day was nearly gone, so he got dressed and left to go to see Kung Fo for another hit.

When he got there, Kung Fo wasn't in, got arrested according to the old woman. What for she couldn't tell Ricky, as she didn't know herself. Disappointed, and craving anything that would fuck him up, he left in search of a new dealer.

4

He found himself back in New Soho. Down the dark alleys he searched, for anyone who was holding, anything that could help him loosen up. Down one alley he found a Portuguese man who, he thought, looked like Alejandro. Maybe the cravings were making him hallucinate, he wasn't sure.

"You holdin'?" he asked the Alejandro lookalike, the jitters had come on in tidal waves and he was scratching his cheek, why was it all of a sudden so itchy. He must've looked crazy to this guy, but he didn't care. He needed a fix and he needed it now.

"Wha' chu' need man?" the Alejandro lookalike asked.

"Got any Ko Sang?"

"I don' deal tha' chinky shit man."

"Well, what do you have?" the jitters making him stutter.

"Got Golden Brown or Columbian White, only

the classics here man."

"I'll take some Golden Brown."

"Five hundred credits," the Alejandro lookalike said.

Ricky dug deep in his pockets, he'd left his wallet back at the club.

"Aww shit," he said as he pulled his empty, shaking hands out his coat.

"No money, no sale," the Alejandro clone said.

"But I need that shit!"

The Alejandro doppelganger turned to him and pulled out a switchblade. Ricky tried to pull out his gun but that holster was jammed with something. His jitters didn't help either. After a few attempts, much to the delight of the Alejandro twin, he managed to unholster his revolver and attempted to aim, but the cravings took over and he couldn't see straight, let alone aim. Alejandro's twin knocked the gun out of Ricky's hand then lunged at him, digging the blade into his stomach.

He could feel his energy spill out on the ground, along with his blood. He fell to his knees as the Alejandro clone pulled the knife out and left him to die.

After a few minutes, he used the wall to help himself to his feet, he staggered back to the street, his legs nearly giving way to blood loss and Ko Sang cravings. He looked up to the sky, fake birdsong from the loud speakers filled his ears. The government had installed fake birdsong to make New London a little more livable. Suddenly, his eyes glazed over and he fell to the ground.

What felt like days later, he awoke in a white room. He could smell the disinfectant and it made his head swim.

"He's coming round," he heard a voice say.

He tried to rise, but latex hands stopped him. He tried to open his eyes, but the light from the room gave him a stinging sensation. He felt the cannula, the catheter and the colostomy bag.

"Sir?" an American voice said, "don't try to get up, your stitches are still healing, and we found the remnants of Ko Sang in your system, have you been using?"

"Only a little bit," he lied.

"Our evidence proves otherwise, sir."

"Why the fuck did you ask me then?"

"Just a formality."

He went back to sleep.

Hours later, he woke again. There was a man in a suit sitting in the chair beside him, his grey hair slick back with gel. He leaned forward, rested his elbows on the bed and made a pyramid with his fingers.

"Good evening, Ricky," he said, smiling.

"Evening?, it's evening? I can't tell."

"We've been watching you, Ricky, we like to keep tabs on new....entrepreneurs in New Soho," he said.

"What do you want from me?"

"The question is, Ricky," he said, leaning back, linking his fingers and resting his hands on his chest, "what do you want from us?"

"Ko Sang," Ricky said.

"We can get you some of that, no problem, we can get you a lifetime's supply, depending on how long you live of course."

Ricky tried to laugh but the intense pain in his stomach came on in droves.

"Relax," the man in the suit said, "you don't have to laugh at all my jokes."

"There's another thing I want," Ricky said.

"Oh?" the man in the suit asked, "and what is that?"

"I wanna rule New London."

Ricky fell back asleep.

She was stood above him, smiling. His brothers, laying bisected on the ground. Their guts spilled out in little piles at the bottom of their abdomens. Their blood, trickling out across the ground like little rivers. He tried to rise, but she planted her foot on his chest and pushed him back to the ground. Then she was naked, standing there above him like a dominatrix.

He woke up screaming again. The nurses trying to restrain him. In the end, he gave up. He didn't see the point in fighting it anymore. 'Just let go' he thought, and he lay back down.

"What time is it?" he asked one of the nurses. A pretty brunette.

"Almost six in the morning," she replied, "you almost gave us a scare there, you were talking in your sleep, saying something about your brothers?"

"They're dead."

"I'm so sorry."

"It's ok, they had it coming, some people would think…"

"Your stitches have healed, do you want to get up?"

Ricky sat up with only a faint twinge in his stomach.

"That pain should go," the nurse said, "but you can leave today, no major internal injuries, should be sore for a day or two."

He got up and out of bed.

"There's some new clothes," she said, "on the chair for you, some guy in a suit left them."

He looked and saw a black satin suit with red lapels, black shirt and black shoes with red lining inside.

He got dressed and signed himself out of the ward. As he walked, he struggled to find something to do with his hands so he put them in his pockets. He felt something. Some sort of card. He took his hands out and sure enough, it was a card. A calling card it looked like. Bone, with emerald lettering, raised. It said they would call him in a few days and that they'd left a little gift for him back at the Neon Potato.

When he got there, there was indeed a gift waiting for him. A small purple mountain and a new syringe. He sat down in his big chair and cooked, injected and sat back, he let the woes of the world wash away. Hands dancing on his skin again and the vibrations of the music flowing through him.

5

The next day, he was visited in his office by a young woman in mirrorshades. Her PVC bodysuit squeaked and creaked as she walked, her stilettos clicking on the floor with each step she took. He sat up as she entered and rubbed his eyes.

"How can I help you?" he asked.

"My name is Deanna Voss, I'm an associate of Adam Von Croft, the man in the suit who visited you in the hospital, he organised your suit and your Ko Sang."

"Ok, tell him thanks."

"You can tell him yourself, he's organised another treat for you, a Samsung 5000 implant."

Ricky couldn't believe his ears, or his eyes for that matter. This hot number waltzing into his office saying he's got more gifts coming to him? He found himself smiling.

"He knew you'd like the sound of that," she said "you're to go to Dr Davies, he's all prepped and ready for you."

At the back alley surgery, Ricky walked up to the secretary.

"Hi, um, I'm here for the ah...Samsung 5000 implant?"

"Oh Mr Walters!" the secretary said, her smile beaming, "go straight through, Dr Davies is waiting for you."

He walked into the operating room and Dr Davies was indeed there, waiting and grinning his near toothless grin. He tapped the arm of the chair and Ricky walked over and sat down.

"Now," Dr Davies said, "I'll just put you under and we'll do this procedure pronto. I know you're a busy man."

At that, Ricky was put under and experienced something of a dream.

She was again stood over him, in all her naked glory. She began to moan, rubbing herself. Ricky was more puzzled than scared. Why was she doing this? Her hand made its way to her mouth and she licked her fingers. Then she brought her hand down and entered herself. She whimpered meekly and Ricky woke up in the chair.

Once he'd paid and left, Ricky pondered on why his dreams of the Supreme Colony Boss, as she was known then, were becoming increasingly sexual in nature. He hated the bitch so why in the blue hell did he want to fuck her? Maybe it was the drugs. Maybe it was the fact that she was one of the only handful of women on the colony. He didn't know. All he did know was he had to find out what happened at Alejandro's place, he'd been using Ko Sang to procrastinate and now it was time to work.

It was dark now, darker than usual in the neon paradise that was New London. It was as if a dark cloud had passed over the city. His hand vibrated and a jingle rang out, causing some of the passersby to stare. Ricky checked his hand. It was Adam Von Croft. With a flick of his thumb the call was answered.

"Ricky?" Von Croft said, "I need you to come in so we can have a chat, it's about Alejandro."

"Where's 'in'?"

"Go to your club, Deanna is waiting for you."

With that, Von Croft hung up.

The Neon Potato was busier than normal tonight. People grinding to the synthetic beats blasting through the speakers. Blue UV and neon blurring together. He needed a hit. Just enough to get him through the night. Ricky went to his office and Deanna was indeed waiting for him. She was sat on his bed, legs crossed and smoking. She offered him one, but he declined. This puzzled her as he was a Ko Sang user, but he didn't smoke. He sat at his desk and cooked.

"You'll need a clear head for this meeting," she

said, "put the needle down."

He extracted the liquid into the syringe and set it aside for later.

They got to Von Croft's lavish apartment sometime later and he was wearing a burgundy smoking jacket. He was facing his window when they were shown in by the latino maid.

"Hello Ricky, please sit."

Ricky sat on a plush, white silk sofa. He couldn't wait for this meeting to be over so he can go back to his club and get a hit. He was also eager to find out what happened to Alejandro too so he felt a little conflicted. Von Croft turned to him and continued.

"I take it you still don't know what happened to your friend in the slums."

"No," Ricky replied, "all I know is that he killed Tiffany and then himself, but that doesn't sound like him."

"He was killed," Von Croft said, "by an undercover policeman, one, it seems, you have already exacted revenge on."

"David Wright?" Ricky asked.

Von Croft winked and pointed a finger gun at Ricky.

"That's the one."

"How do you know I killed him?"

"Like I said at the hospital," Von Croft said, "we

like to look after our new entrepreneurs, somebody has already been to his apartment to clean up after you so you don't need to worry about that anymore, also we've paid for your other friend, Kung Fo, to be released on good behaviour, so you can still get your Ko Sang, if the supply we gave you runs out."

"Ok," Ricky said, his hands in the air, "what's the catch?"

"The catch is," Von Croft said, "we want you to push our new drug in your club, one that's been expertly crafted in our lab."

"Who exactly are you though?" Ricky asked.

"We are the ones who wait and watch in the shadows," Deanna said finally, after being quiet all the way from the club.

"You'll have to excuse Deanna," Von Croft said, "she has a penchant for dramatics, we're a conglomerate, made up of all the major corporations and their affiliates in the city. We're the big leagues boy. You wanted to own the city? This is the best way to do it."

"What about Big Tito?"

"He's already been dealt with, he shouldn't bother you anymore."

An hour later, Ricky was back in his office, taking a hit of his beloved Ko Sang. Deanna was still with him, sat on the bed. She began to undress, and lay naked on the purple silk sheets. Her hair, cut in a bob, matched the colour of the bed and, throwing her mirrorshades on the bedside table, she beckoned to him. He walked over and she undressed him. They made love until the sun came up and Ricky never felt any happier.

6

It was the next morning, and Ricky was watching Deanna sleep. It was in the light of the sun that he noticed her cat-like eyes. The way they curved up in the outer corners. Then they were open and green. He traced her arm with his fingertips and smiled. And she smiled back. Her lips, not too thin and not too fat, parted slightly. It was that perfect moment where no words were said. No words needed to be said. Just, simply, perfect. Suddenly, last night's hit wore off and he walked, naked, over to his desk and cooked. Just as he was injecting, Deanna walked over, naked also, and put her arms around him. He suddenly jolted upright and yelled at her.

"DON'T TOUCH ME WHILE I'M TAKING A HIT!!!"

It was then, the perfect moment had ended and, pissed off, she got dressed and left, leaving Ricky to experience his high alone. No music, no whores, no UV lights, no neon. Just him in the awful light of the sun.

Hours later, he felt terrible. How could he have just snapped at her? He tried her number. No answer. So he called Von Croft. He hadn't seen her all day. Ricky got dressed and left the club in search of her. There was a heavy police presence in the street. Ricky had never trusted the police. But he stopped and asked them what happened.

"Woman got stabbed," the nearest officer said, "took her to the hospital in New Hampstead."

"What did she look like?" Ricky asked.

"Purple-"

Ricky didn't need to hear the rest of the description. He flagged down an empty taxi pod and it took him to New Hampstead Medical Centre.

New Hampstead was quite affluent, just like its original. And it had the best healthcare in New London. It was where Ricky was brought when he got stabbed, so he was full of hope as they pulled in and he paid the taxi. He rushed to the reception.

"Deanna Voss?" he asked.

"Room two-three-four, second floor," the receptionist said, slightly disinterested in her job, it seemed.

As he got to the second floor, his hand vibrated. It was Von Croft.

"Deanna's been stabbed," he said, when his hologram burst out of Ricky's hand.

"I know," Ricky said, "I'm in the hospital now, I'm going to see her."

"Ok," Von Croft said, "let me know how she is."

"Will do," Ricky said, and hung up.

He got to room two-three-four and saw her there. Hooked up to god knows what. She was asleep and he didn't want to wake her, so he just sat by her and waited. Going over their last conversation in his head. Now he really felt bad for snapping at her.

A few hours later, she woke up and Ricky jumped at the chance to apologise for yelling at her. Then his hand vibrated and Von Croft popped up again.

"How is she?"

"She's just woke up," Ricky replied.

"I have some welcome news, we know who stabbed her."

"Who?"

"The same fucker who stabbed you, I've arranged for my men to be at his apartment in the high rise quarter in five minutes."

"Tell them to fall back," Ricky said, "I've got this."

The high rise quarter was like the Portuguese slums, but in a different part of the city. Filled with gangs, each have their own mega block to patrol. The slums were rough, but the high rise quarter was rougher. The crime rate dwarfed that of the slums, with a crime happening every ten minutes. When Ricky got there, Von Croft's men were just getting out of their armoured pods. Armed to the teeth with superior firepower.

"Lemme get one of those," he said to a huge guy in black, blue and grey camo wear, who smiled and gave him a revolver and ten bullets. They knew who he was because Von Croft had informed them before he got there. Ricky smiled when he opened the gun and found it was already loaded.

"So which block are we looking at?" he asked the big guy.

"Block twenty," the big guy replied.

They took the streets with caution. Who knew who was scoping them through the lens of a sniper rifle. They got to block twenty in about ten minutes, in two by two cover formation. It was run down and the elevators weren't working so they had to take the stairs.

A guard on the fifth floor was patrolling the barely lit corridors. It'd been a bad day for him, first his mother had kicked him out for gangbanging, then he had to pay her rent, then his girlfriend dumped him and now he was on shitty guard duty on the fifth floor. He hated the fifth floor. Dirty and it smelled funny. But he'd heard that someone put a hit out on the boss's nephew for stabbing people in New Soho again, When will that kid ever learn?, so here he was, fifth floor and hungry. As he was making a sweep of the east corridor, he saw a squad of camo guys and a skinny fucker in a long coat making their way up the stairs. He opened fire and ducked for cover in the frame of the nearest door. They did also and a firefight ensued. They exchanged fire for a few minutes until he clicked empty.

"Shit," he said under his breath.

When the firefight had stopped, Ricky hadn't even pulled the trigger once. The hit squad had done all the shooting thus far. They heard the welcome click of the guard's empty clip. Each one of them smiled to one another and broke cover. The guard broke cover too and ran for the stairs at the opposite end of the east corridor. One of the hit squad guys then shot him in the back and he went down like a sack of shit.

As he hit the floor, the guard's life flashed before his eyes. What had he done with the existence he was given? Nothing but gangbanging, drugs and women. The last thing he saw was his blood, pooling a circle around where he lay.

They carried on up the stairs. Room eight-four-three on the eighth floor. That's where the little bastard lived.

"Not for long," Ricky found himself saying, as

though he was following a thought verbally.

They got to the eighth floor in five minutes. There were guards outside the room and all along the corridors. They had to be quiet if they wanted to get out of this alive so they connected silencers to their rifles and crept along the corridor walls, picking off guards as they went. Ricky followed the pros and soon they got to the door to room eight-four-three. With most of the guards dead, they removed the silencers from their rifles.

"Now," the front hit squader said, turning to the others, "there's two on the door, we take them out, bust in, secure the area but Ricky gets the kid, ok?"

They all nodded in acknowledgment and, with military precision, dispatched the guards in a flurry of superior gunfire. The big guy kicked the door down and they all piled in, Ricky following quickly behind.

The kid was sitting on a leather sofa with two of his 'bitches' either side of him, smoking heroin and drinking imported vodka. Ricky bet he only had the finest shit to give him a sense of grandeur. It didn't work. As soon as he saw Ricky, he was on his knees begging not to die. But Ricky had other plans. He aimed his revolver at the kid and opened fire, blowing the kid's head up. Alejandro's twin won't be stabbing, or selling drugs to, anyone ever again. Which made Ricky feel a little sad.

PART 2:

Snakes and Ladders

7

It was a few days later that Deanna was let out of hospital, and Ricky went to pick her up. He was on a high from Ko Sang that meant he could function normally. She wasn't best pleased, but he was there at least. She got into his brand new Ford Electric 40 pod and they lifted off. As they flew through the bustling metropolis of New London, the sun shone through the window and onto Ricky's arm as he had it hanging, leisurely, out the window. They got to a set of traffic lights and his hand vibrated. He flicked his thumb then moved his hand to the dashboard. The hologram of Von Croft popped up next to the speedometer.

"How can I help, Von Croft?"

"I trust Deanna is with you and safe?"

"Yeah," Ricky replied, "we're on our way to see you now, should be-" he checks the clock, "five minutes."

The lights turn green, and traffic starts to move.

"I'll see you soon," Von Croft said, and his

hologram disappeared.

Ricky turned to Deanna and smiled.

At Von Croft's, they sat down on the sofa as Von Croft paced the room.

"I don't understand," he said, he stops pacing and is now looking out the window, "the shipment came in, why isn't it here for distribution?"

"Do you want me to check it out?" Ricky asked.

"Us," Deanna said, "we'll check it out."

"No, Deanna," said Von Croft, "you need rest, you've just come out of hospital for a very nasty injury. Ricky will do it."

At that, Ricky nodded and left.

"Where the fuck is this shipment area?" Ricky said, under his breath, as he searched the factory floor just outside New Battersea. Electric pods were flying everywhere, carrying goods to different areas of New London, food, provisions etc.

He spotted a short, fat man in high vis and a hardhat wearing glasses.

"Where's Von Croft's goods?" he asked him.

"Von Croft?"

"Yeah," Ricky said, "Adam Von Croft, very important man, where's his goods?"

At that the short, fat man knew what Ricky was talking about, but told him that it hadn't arrived yet.

Someone must've intercepted it, Ricky thought,

but where to start looking for it?

He got in his electric pod and lifted off.

The pod's onboard computer told him that CCTV showed the shipment had been intercepted somewhere near the airspace over the Portuguese slums, so he flew south. When he got there, he landed and got out, locked the door up tight, though he knew it wouldn't stop anyone here from trying to jack a brand new Ford. He asked a beggar if he saw any pods with shipments landing anywhere near here.

"For the right amount of credits," the vagrant said, "I'll see anything."

"How much?"

"Fifty, need to get me some liquor."

"Fine."

Ricky gave the beggar fifty credits and he told him that he saw a few pods going towards the warehouses near the back of the slums. Ricky kind of knew where they were so he set off to find them.

When he got there, he saw the place was heavily guarded, so he found some cover by a pile of old crates. He screwed a silencer onto his revolver. He didn't want a full blown firefight, there were too many armed guards around. But also he didn't want to leave his pod too long in this place. Then it would almost certainly be jacked. One of the guards left his post momentarily, Ricky took his chance and aimed, fired, and caught the remaining guard in the head. Suddenly, the jitters came and Ricky really needed a hit. He didn't bring any Ko Sang with him.

"Shit," he said under his breath.

He took a deep breath and tried to focus.

Then he heard a shout.

The other guard!

To avoid attention, he steadied himself and aimed again.

He dispatched the guard and ran towards the warehouse door, pressing himself up against the wall and opening the door carefully, looked around. There were huge pods inside. The shipment must be in one of these, for sure.

The warehouse walls were made of corrugated iron, along one side were some gasoline tanks that could be blown up if need be. He rang Von Croft and told him everything.

"Can you get to the pods?" Von Croft asked.

"Yeah," Ricky said, "but what about my Ford?"

"I'll send someone to pick it up."

"Ok," he said, and hung up.

Ricky looked up and saw a huge opening in the roof. That's how they got the pods in.

He crept in and hid behind some boxes. An unsuspecting guard walked past and Ricky shot him point blank in the head. Creeping through the labyrinth of boxes, Ricky took out a few more guards with military precision. He was amazed how well he could shoot with the cravings slowly becoming the only thing he can think about.

He soon got to the pods. They were guarded by two men with AK47s. He wondered how he could take one out without alerting the other. Then the cravings inside told him "fuck it" and he removed the silencer. There was going to be a firefight whatever he did. Suddenly the jitters were followed by double, blurred vision and weak knees. God, he needed a hit. Just one. Doesn't have to be a strong one. Just enough to get his faculties back. There could be some Ko Sang on the pods, if only there was a way to connect them. That way he could tow the other one out with him when he took off. He made for the pods, making sure he kept out of the guard's line of sight. When he got there, his vision had improved slightly and he noticed there were attachments to either side of the pod, so you could tow something if need be. He climbed a ladder and pulled some tow cables out, connecting the two pods together. Then he climbed inside one of the pods, no keys in the ignition.

"Shit," he found himself saying out loud.

Out of the corner of his eye, he saw a sectioned off room in the corner, it looked like a cloakroom of some sort. Climbing gently and quietly down from the huge pod, he made his way towards the room, taking and breaking cover as he did so, to keep out of sight of the guards.

As he got to the room, he took cover and snuck through the place, squatting so the other guards wouldn't see him.

"Who the fuck are you?"

He tensed, and turned to see a black man in high vis and hardhat.

"I'm the safety inspector," Ricky lied.

"Safety inspector?!"

Ricky hushed him with a hand on his mouth and, pressing his gun to the man's gut asked "where's the fucking keys to the fucking pods?"

The black man, obviously nervous, pointed to the chipboard above the desk in the corner. There, hanging under a yellow light, in all its glory, were the keys. Ricky knocked the guy out with the handle of his revolver and retrieved the keys.

As he walked out, he thought "fuck cover, fuck the AKs, I'm taking these fucking pods."

He walked straight up to the pods, gun at the ready, but the guards were nowhere to be seen. Then he heard someone calling for reinforcements and realised that he didn't have time to waste. So he quickly climbed inside the pod and started the engine. To his left and right, he saw guards running over and firing their weapons at him. He stuck his arm out the window and laid down some cover fire as he took off out of the roof, dragging the second pod behind him.

8

Flying over New London, he saw his pod parked on the roof of the apartment building that Von Croft owned, and breathed a sigh of relief. He landed safely next to it and got out. The old bastard better have some Ko Sang on him or nearby. The cravings making his head spin, he vomited on the flower bed, and as soon as he looked up from the bile, last night's curry and the geraniums, he saw Deanna.

"Hey," he said.

"Charming," she said back.

In his office, Von Croft was eager to see Ricky and find out what happened to his shipment.

He turned as Ricky and Deanna entered.

"My shipment?"

"Safely on the roof," Ricky said, "my Ko Sang?"

Von Croft smiled.

"Safely in your club office."

Ricky felt relieved.

He got back to his club just as the sun was going

down, finding a huge purple mountain on his desk. Without wasting any time he cooked, took a hit and lay down on his bed. The club was full tonight, which made him feel extra good. Deanna came in and lay next to him, already naked, and they made love.

Hours later, laying bathed in each other's sweat, Ricky was on the verge of sleep when the music on the dancefloor stopped. Gunfire and screams rose like an instant hit of a crescendo. Pulling up his skinny jeans, Ricky grabbed his revolver, loaded it and looked outside his office. Deanna was sat up in bed and Ricky motioned her to stay there. He peeped out and saw several armed men walking along the dancefloor. He ran out and took cover behind the bar, where the barman was cowering and crying.

"Man up," he said to the barman, "or you lose your job."

He peeked over the bar, right into the smiling face of Big Tito.

Big Tito grabbed him by the neck with his new muscle grafted arm, wires still connected to his brain via cables in his neck, and squeezed. Ricky pulled them out again and Big Tito dropped him and scrambled to reconnect them as Ricky got his breath back. Ricky stood up to face gun barrels pointing at him. He was screwed. His hand vibrated. Von Croft.

"I need to take this," he said, and Big Tito nodded to say ok.

He flicked his thumb and suddenly ten armed men burst through the door, firing corporate bought, military grade weapons. Big Tito ran for the back exit and escaped, while the others were shot and killed. Their blood, black in the blue UV lighting. Ricky looked over to his office door to see a naked Deanna, smiling and holding a phone. He heard Von Croft's voice from his hand and lifted it to see the hologram of his saviour, popping up and flickering.

"I trust you're safe now?"

"I have you to thank for the intervention?"

"But of course," Von Croft said, "we like to look after you."

The next morning, Ricky woke with a start. Dreams of Big Tito and gun barrels fading in the rising sunlight. He walked over to his desk and cooked. His hands trembling with anticipation. This was going to be a good hit. Deanna turned over and stretched like a cat in her sleep. He decided, that day, he was going to visit Kung Fo. Aside from being his dealer, Kung Fo was also a dear friend. He was also a dab hand at computers and getting information on people quite quickly. Once the hit was underway and he could function,

Ricky got dressed and went to the roof where his pod was parked.

Flying over New London at this time of day was hectic. People going to work, school, or, like Ricky, visiting friends. In traffic, Ricky was listening to the radio. His favorite track was on, so he didn't so much dance as moved in a fashion that made it look like he either needed the toilet or he was trying to get comfy. The sun beamed through the window and onto his hands on the steering pad and Ricky felt its warmth pulse through him like soft hands caressing his skin. He didn't know if it was the Ko Sang or the fact it was a warm day, but Ricky felt good.

"You wan' product?" Kung Fo smiled as Ricky came through the door of the shop.

"Not today, I have a new supplier," Ricky said, "but I do need info on an Adam Von Croft and a Deanna Voss."

"Ok, give me….two hour, then i have info for you, in the meantime, you wan' new product?"

"New product?"

"Yeah," Kung Fo said, "it called fuck you," they both laughed.

Two hours later, Kung Fo called Ricky into the back room where he kept all his hardware. He certainly did have info on Von Croft and Deanna. He read aloud.

"Adam Von Croft, born 2/12/83, geez he's old, served in Afghanistan 2/11/03 to 25/2/06, honourable discharge, served two years for smuggling upon return to the UK, set up business after that, it doesn't say what business he set up."

"That because," Kung Fo said, smiling now, "it government product."

"Government product?"

"Yeah," Kung Fo turned back to the computer, "not much on Deanna Voss, sorry."

"Wait a second, how do you know it was a government product?"

"It Von Croft, next to Harold Butters, he was biggest pusher in New London but no way of tracing where it came from, so in my thinking, government. Sometime I forget you on prison colony, I sorry."

Ricky had a lot to think about on his flight back to New Soho. He didn't want to be messing with government business. In the scheme of things, he was small fry. The sun had gone by the time he got back to the club and the rain had started.

"You ok?" Deanna asked as he got to the office, she was wearing her black PVC bodysuit and black stilettos, "you look like you've seen a ghost."

At that, the air raid sirens blared out, an acid rain storm was on its way. It'd been a few weeks since the last one, the heat wave was over and now it was mother nature's payback.

"I've been doing some digging on Von Croft," Ricky admitted, a little tentative as he did so, he didn't want to spook her.

Failed. She was the one who'd looked like she saw a ghost now.

"And?" she asked.

"I found out he was a big guy in the drugs business."

"And you're alarmed because?"

"Because I'm a small guy, I'm no dealer, I'm a buyer."

"What did you get sent down for again?"

"Murder and drugs charges."

"Again," she said, one hand on her hip, "you're alarmed because?"

"It's government business."

"So?" she said, "you get your poison of choice, whenever you want it, you get me, again, whenever you want it," she winked at him and walked over, getting close and stroking his cheek, "where's the problem?"

"I suppose you're right," he conceded.

Hours later, he awoke from a sleep he didn't remember going for. It was dark and the rain pitter pattered on his window. Its shadow on the wall illuminated by the blue neon of the sign for the club outside. No one had been to party since the shoot out, which was bad for business. Very bad. He walked over to his desk and cooked. It was then, he realised he was alone. Deanna had vanished. He took a hit and leaned back in his chair. Maybe she was in the toilets washing up? Maybe she'd gone out to get some food? He didn't know, and at that time, didn't care. It was a big hit. He regretted digging around on someone who'd taken care of his every need, saved his life, helped him keep the club. He lifted his hand to call Von Croft to admit what he'd done, but as he did so, his hand vibrated anyway. His flicked his thumb inwards and Von Croft popped up.

"I'm very disappointed in you Ricky," he said, "I did all in my power to help you and you do this? If you wanted to know anything you could've just asked, I'm an open book to my associates. Unfortunately when I get disappointed I also get angry," the front windows crashed through and several men in camouflage and holding big military grade rifles burst into the room, Ricky quickly hid under his desk as bullets spat in his direction, "it's no use, you'll be dead in five minutes."

He reached for his revolver in his desk drawer and hung up on Von Croft.

He waited for the armed men to click empty, now was his time. He rose up from his cover and fired, taking them all out without having to load once. He called Von Croft back.

"Is that the best you got?"

Von Croft looked surprised.

"You seem to be harder to kill than I thought, but not to worry, I have eyes, ears and guns everywhere, watch your back Ricky."

9

He decided it wasn't safe to stay in the club, nor was it safe to carry this Samsung 5000 implant in his hand. He got dressed and left, taking a small bag of Ko Sang with him for later. The small bag felt heavy in his trench coat pocket, so did his gun, but he felt safe knowing they were there. Walking the streets, (he couldn't use his pod as no doubt it was bugged to know his every move), he soon felt eyes watching him. A man in a grey suit and grey fedora was talking into his wrist and staring at him. A woman looking at him through her compact mirror as she applied make up. The homeless guy with barely any teeth, seemingly talking to himself. Down the street, and the waiter for an outdoor cafe stopped pouring coffee for an elderly couple as he walked past, and stared at him. The elderly couple were watching him too. Is this what Von Croft meant about eyes, ears and guns everywhere? Or is it too much Ko Sang? He didn't know for sure, but what he did know, was that he wasn't safe in this town anymore. Fuck owning the city, now he just wanted to survive it.

He walked into the back alley surgery and Dr Davies was just closing up for the night.

"Doc," Ricky said, "I need you to take this phone out of my hand."

"Sorry son," he said, "I'm closed, you'll have to come back in the morning."

"But you don't understand I need this out now!"

Dr Davies sighed and opened the shutters again, the loud clanging hurting Ricky's ears and signifying that Dr Davies wasn't pleased with this intrusion on his private time.

Hours later, his hand stinging slightly, Ricky was in the Portuguese slums, walking towards Alejandro's caravan. He decided to hide out here for a while, where, he thought, he'd be best safe. He entered the caravan, and felt a buckshot in his chest. It knocked him backwards and out the door, a giant cloud of blood coloured Ko Sang blooming in his wake. He coughed blood as he squirmed on the ground.

"Hell yeah!" a voice shouted, "bounty's mahne!"

People gathered round the commotion. Ricky sat up to see a young-ish looking guy with a smoking shotgun barrel aimed right at him. He reached for his revolver and the young man said "ah ah ah! Easy now, don't wanna mess up mah shoes now do we? Ahm suprahsed yew can git up after that buckshot."

Quickly, Ricky unholstered his gun and took out the kids kneecaps. The kid writhed in pain on the floor.

"Now tell me about this bounty," he panted, standing over the kid.

"Old man Von Croft," the kid screamed, "put a bounty on yer hayd, said a million credits for yew dayd."

"Well," Ricky said, lifting up the kid's shotgun and wincing in pain, "you're out a million," and shot him in the head.

He stumbled through the streets, his sight becoming blurry with blood loss, he had to find a medical centre, and quick. It wasn't long until he found one and he collapsed in the A&E waiting room. Nurses gathering around him.

Hours later he woke up in fresh linen. Big Tito leaning over and smiling. He screamed and threw the bedsheet at him and stumbled out of the bed. Big Tito was gone. It was a morphine dream. He stood up and felt hands guiding him into his bed. The nurse was saying how surprised she was he was still alive and that it was touch and go for a while. Once he was settled and under his bed sheet again, he fell back asleep. The morphine running through his veins like a stream.

A day later, he was checking himself out of the centre, much to the doctor's advice not to. They did, however, give him some morphine to take if the pain got too much. As he left, he was grasped by the lapels of his trench coat and dragged into an alleyway. It was Deanna, her hair was blue now.

"I'm so sorry," she was saying, "I had no idea Von Croft was gonna put a bounty on you, or I wouldn't have told him you dug around on him."

"So it's you I gotta thank for that wake up call?"

"Yes, I'm so sorry."

"Well, life hasn't been quiet, I'll tell you that."

Suddenly she glanced upwards.

"What's wrong?" he asked.

"He's got drones," she said, "out looking for you."

She looked back at him and smiled.

"We're safe, but for how long I don't know," she said.

They walked into the street, hanging onto one another like a pair of young lovers, trying to blend in with the crowd on the street, every so often glancing upwards, looking for drones.

10

They got to her rented apartment not long after. It was dark and the shadows of the moving traffic of pods outside were dancing on the walls. Neon flickered on her face as she dropped Ricky on a chair by the window.

"Take a nap," she ordered as she went to the kitchenette and poured a glass of water, first for herself, then for him.

"I slept enough at the medical centre," he said.

"Rest a while then," she said, slightly exasperated.

The pain came back so he reached into his pocket and dug out one of the syringes of morphine he got from the doctors. He looked at it in the dark blue light and half smiled. They were really trusting to give him, a known drug addict, takeaway morphine. He injected into his arm and sat back to relax.

It was in the early morning light that he saw the place for what it was, a dump. Clothes strewn across the floor, dirty dishes on the counter and bed. Her phone rang. Ricky was in two minds whether or not to answer as this wasn't his home, but she slept the sleep of the dead and the sound was annoying him.

"Hello?" he said into the receiver.

"Ricky," said the voice on the other end, they let the name roll off the tongue, savouring the very last syllable. His eyes shot open wide when he realised it was Von Croft.

"The kid didn't kill you I suppose," Von Croft said, "not to worry, there's a few drones headed your way, if you hurry you might just be able to catch them."

It was then Ricky saw a red spot on the wall by the phone. Von Croft started laughing down the phone. The red spot moved from the wall to the phone, up the line, to the receiver, then there was an explosion as the window shattered and the phone blew up, taking Ricky's last two fingers with it. He ducked out of the way and three drones piled in through the window in single file. Deanna woke up and screamed.

"It wasn't supposed to be like this!!" she was saying, and Ricky felt a bit confused. What was it supposed to be like then? He reached for his gun but it was missing. He looked over to

Deanna, who looked over at the dresser by

her bed. His eyes followed hers and he saw his revolver. Dodging the fire from the drones they both ran for the gun. He got there first and, with his gun grasped in his hand, he jumped out the window. He free-fell for a second or two before landing on the roof of a pod, startling a shocked family inside. He clambered up and saw the three drones in hot pursuit. Had Deanna been on special orders to detain him until the drones had arrived? Why would she betray him? The three drones had caught up with them at a traffic light so Ricky, spotting another pod below them starting to move, jumped off and landed on the second pod's roof. He noticed an open window to his right, so he jumped off the pod and entered the building, startling the old Japanese woman who was using a sewing machine. The drones followed him, firing. He ran through the front door and found himself in a long corridor. Turning right, he ran fast down to a corner where he turned and looked to see if the drones were following him. The front one was looking down the opposite end of the corridor so he hid.

"Shit," he said under his breath.

The cravings started to kick in again. The morphine had worked for a little while but that was wearing off, so he dug around his pockets again, and, producing another syringe, injected the sweet morphine into his system.

He squatted down and fell asleep in the corridor.

He woke up to a whirring sound. He saw a camera lens zoom in on him.

"Hello, Ricky," a voice from a microphone said. The drones had found him. The front one prepared to open fire, and Ricky rolled out of the way just in time and, rolling onto his back, he aimed and opened fire. Three shots and the first one was down. Two more shots on the second one and he clicked empty. He got up and ran for his life towards a window at the opposite end of the corridor. He jumped through it and landed in sewage. 'That's right' he thought, 'I'm by the sewage line'. He got up out the gutter and dug around his coat for ammunition, found four more bullets, and loaded, all the while keeping out of sight of the drones. He edged his way along the side of the gutter until he came to a ledge. He peered down and saw the colony below him. He was at the edge of New London. Surely the drones wouldn't follow him here?

The ledge followed round to the right and Ricky pressed himself to the wall and walked tentatively along the edge. The rain had made the ledge slick and slippery and Ricky stumbled a few times, but he made his way to an alcove which had a greyish green door that said "authorised personnel only" in huge red letters. He entered and found himself in a large room, a boiler room of sorts. Gun aimed, he made his way through the labyrinth of pipes and valves until he came to another door with a red light shining above it. He tried the handle. Locked. So he shot it and it fell to the floor, clanging loud enough to wake the dead. Pushing it open, he saw a staircase, running up several floors, with a door at each landing. He walked to the top floor and tried the handle of that door. It was open. Gun at the ready, he opened it with a loud screech, and found himself on a street corner. High rise apartments towered above him and he realised he'd seen these streets before.

11

Ricky was never normally a nervous person, but in the high rise quarter, it paid to be a little nervous. He holstered his revolver, put his hands in his pockets and walked along the slick, wet pavement. He was hungry now, but he realised there weren't any restaurants in the high rise quarter. There was too high a chance of them getting robbed. The high rise quarter was built to house the undesirables of the undesirables. The ones who, if they weren't serving time on the colony, would run amok as the police would very rarely show themselves here. Drugs, gambling, women, you name it, they did it here. It was so bad not even people from New Soho or the slums would come down here. They were very territorial in the high rise quarter too. If they didn't know you, they viewed you with suspicion, and most likely try to kill you.

He started as he heard gunshots, a kid ran out of a pawn shop with trails of money flowing behind him. Next to the pawn shop however was a gun shop, Never Click Empty, Ricky needed more ammo so he went in. He was greeted by a dark room, lit only by neon lights advertising different guns and hunting getaways. Not like anyone here could afford them, but they looked like nice dreams for people here to fantasise about while they rotted in their thirtieth floor shit houses.

"Haven't seen you before, just moved here?" the cashier asked.

"Um, yeah kinda," Ricky replied.

"What can I do ya for?"

"I need more ammo for this,"

"Woah!" said the cashier, hand out as if he didn't want to see it, "don't flash that thing here."

"Why? What's wrong?"

The cashier pointed at a CCTV camera above the desk.

"Some people might think you're trying to rob me."

"Oh," Ricky said, and put his gun away.

"Just by looking at it," the cashier said, "I can tell it's a colt and we don't do ammo for colts anymore, but if you'd like to part exchange for a newer gun, we can do that."

"Let me see what you've got," Ricky said, and the cashier looked behind the counter at the wide array of guns. Rifles, pistols, crossbows, shotguns, he had everything. Ricky spotted a pistol that he especially liked the look of. It was a newer looking one. He pointed at it and the cashier's eyes lit up.

"Ah the new Beretta six twenty three," he said and took it down from its shelf, "runs on batteries not clips, charges every fifteen shots and uses your body's own electrical current to charge the battery," he pointed it at the ceiling to display it fully to Ricky, "you can see how many shots you got left before charging on this little screen here," he pointed at a small screen with digitised numbers on it situated on the handle of the gun, "all the power of a colt, no worrying about loading all the time. Extra features include a sensor along the barrel that can sense the surroundings, detect any threat, and act accordingly using an on board computer"

"I'll take it," Ricky said.

Back out on the street, Ricky walked cautiously along the wet pavement and came to a square of sorts. Covered by the shadow of the surrounding buildings, it gave off an unending twilight vibe. There was a statue of a fish in the centre, blowing water and looking like it was flicking its tail to escape a fisherman's grasp. Ricky couldn't tell what species it was for the graffiti all over the body. Sat by this statue was a group of youths. All hooded and some practicing wheelies on their push bikes. Ricky paid them no mind and walked with his head down, past them and their 'I'm a gangster' image. They probably were, or thought they were, gangsters, but Ricky had defended himself against bigger and tougher guys down on the colony, so he wasn't really intimidated.

"Hey knob head!" one of them shouted, but Ricky kept on walking.

"Yeah that's it," another one yelled.

Ricky knew if he opened fire on one of them they'd probably scatter like leaves on a breeze, then probably get their relatives, who were in one of the many gangs, to come and hunt him down and try to kill him.

Ricky got to the end of the high rise quarter. He was relieved he'd survived it. He knew though, that Von Croft wasn't going to let him go that easily. His new beretta, safe and snug in his pocket, he walked. The morphine was wearing off so he found an alleyway, away from cameras and the threat of drones, and shot up. It was his last one so he knew he'd have to go to the medical centre and ask for more. Whether or not they'd give him more was up to them. Them and his beretta if they said no. Was he really going to hold up a medical centre though? Had it really come to that? Did he have a problem? He sat against the wet, graffiti ridden wall and felt sleepy. His head lolled back as the morphine washed over him.

He hadn't dreamed in a while, but when he did it was crazy. He was back on the colony. She stood over him, naked and touching herself again. Then Deanna was there, naked also, massaging her breasts and moaning.

He awoke with a start, the air raid sirens were blaring to signify that acid rain was on its way. He ran for an info booth to find the nearest shelter. He found one that was a few blocks away so he ran for his life down the street and found one. As he got there, he was suddenly grabbed by the collar. Thinking it was someone trying to get into the shelter before him he shouted "fuck off!" but he was thrown backwards and into the street. Big Tito was looming above him.

"Your old boss hired me to take you out mother fucker, and I intend to do so."

Ricky struggled to his feet and Big Tito grabbed him again and threw him against a wall. He got up and Big Tito uppercutted him in the stomach, raising him from the ground a few inches. Winded, he got up.

"You just don't learn do ya," Big Tito said, "big guys always win in the end, ya see? I've had an upgrade since we last met," he flexed his new upgraded grafted muscle, "and you're

fucked."

He punched him in the chest, and Ricky felt a

crack, and suddenly it was hard to breath. Big Tito grabbed him by the neck and started to choke him.

"Now you're mine, I'm gonna kill you now!"

Ricky tried for the wiring in the neck but there was none there. Just as the last bit of life was leaving him, Ricky felt a drop of burning on his face. The acid rainstorm was starting. Ricky aimed at Big Tito's chest and fired. Big Tito's smile dropped, and he retreated backwards, letting go of Ricky's throat. Gasping for breath, Ricky then got up, another burning drop of acid rain hit his scalp. He ran for the cover of the shelter and, turning back to see Big Tito, saw him start to melt, like a plastic toy in the microwave. He didn't scream, so much as moaned in pain as he became a brown, pink sludge puddle in the street.

12

He waited for the acid rain to stop before leaving the shelter. The remnants of Big Tito flowing down the drain and into the sewer system.

"Didn't escape that, fucko," he said.

The sun started to evaporate the acid rain and steam rose as he walked along the street. It was time he paid his old boss, Adam Von Croft, a little visit.

PART 3:

Every Working Man's Dream

13

He got to the apartment building, Von Croft Tower, shortly after. He didn't take the bus pod, or drive, he walked. Through the Portuguese slums, through the high rise quarter, where nobody got in his way. The tower was being guarded by Von Croft's elite squad, the guys from the high rise operation where he killed the kid. They were carrying the rifles he saw them use in his club when Big Tito tried to take the Neon Potato back. He was carrying his smart pistol. "Like bows and arrows against the lightning," he remembered from a book he read as a teenager, between getting high, getting laid, and hanging out with Alejandro. Ricky took cover behind a bronze, rusted, and generally fucked up due to acid rain, statue of Von Croft. He was smiling, laughing almost with a group of kids and Ricky felt slightly uneasy. If only the people of this town knew, really knew, what Von Croft was up to behind the closed doors of his apartment. There would be blood in the streets. He watched the guard squad pacing round the building, following their own footsteps. When he'd learned their routes, he struck. He took off his shoes and unlaced them in the alleyway running down the side of the building, good garrotting material. In the shadows of the now setting sun and rising moon, he crept, shoeless and cold, behind a guard and, quickly, quietly, wrapped the shoelace around the man's neck, turned, and lifted him over his shoulder to strangle him. He then dragged the dead guy deeper into the alley and dumped the body in a dumpster.

Suddenly, to the right of him, a guard came out of the fire exit door, saw Ricky, and they had a staring match for a few seconds. Each was equally surprised to see the other. The guard's cigarette, which was, up to this point, dangling lazily from his mouth, left his lips and hit the floor. Everything went in slow motion, the guard lifted his rifle, Ricky lifted his pistol, he would've used the dead guard's rifle but it was too loud, and they had a standoff. The pistol, sensing the situation and the gravity of what would happen should Ricky be discovered by the rest of the squad, throbbed in his hand as it scanned the surroundings and automatically deployed a silencer to the end of the barrel. Impressed, Ricky pulled the trigger, the only sound was the wet splatter of blood and brain matter hitting the now closed fire exit door. He looked at his gun closely and couldn't be more impressed with the silencer. If he ever survives this, he'll give a good review on the shop's website.

He relaced his shoes and put them back on. His feet squelched as he did so and he winced at how much noise they were making. All the slime and grime from the floor had soaked through his socks and it didn't feel pleasant. Once his shoes were on, he made his way through the fire exit and came to a corridor, lit only by a flickering light in the centre of the ceiling, its walls, cold and greyish green. There were coloured lines along the floor going in the direction of the door he just came through. He stalked along the wall, making sure his pistol was up and ready. He came to the end of the corridor and saw that it opened up to a parking garage, populated by expensive looking electric pods. Owned by Von Croft probably. He saw a camera phone booth in the opposite corner so he crept forward slightly only to see a guard patrolling in between each pod. 'Only one?' Ricky thought, then he saw another making his way down the pathway through the car park level. He retreated back a few steps as the guard got closer. He tapped on the wall to get the guard's attention and he dove into the shadows behind a pod. The guard took a look down the corridor and Ricky pulled the trigger, killing the guard instantly. He crept round the pods until he came to the second guard, who he dispatched with expert precision. Ricky reached the camera phone booth and dialled for Kung Fo.

14

Kung Fo was on his computer. His mother said he'd go blind if he stared at that thing long enough. He didn't care, he'd rather go blind than deaf. If he went deaf, he wouldn't be able to listen to the kick ass music blasting from his speakers built into the headrest of his computer chair. Then again, if he went blind, he wouldn't be able to work. So it was a catch twenty two situation. He didn't hear the camera phone at first, but on the fifth ring, he turned the music off and answered.

"Fo?" it was Ricky.

"Ah Ricky," he said, "my main man, you wan' product?"

"No," Ricky said, "I mean yes, I don't know, I'm in trouble."

Ricky proceeded to tell him everything that happened in one long, drawn out, panicked sentence.

"Wha' you wan' Kung Fo to do?" he said, after Ricky had finished.

"I want you to get in your pod and fly up to the roof of Von Croft Tower and pick me up in about," Ricky looked at his watch, "half an hour."

"Ok," Kung Fo said, " but you owe me double for product."

"Ok, ok, just get here," Ricky said, and hung up.

Kung Fo gathered his things and went up to the roof of his mother's shop, his pod was waiting for him there. So was Tsang Su, the local bad seed. He was known to Kung Fo as he procured the Ko Sang from him and they'd normally split the profits from whatever sales they made that day. Kung Fo had missed a payment, and Tsang Su wasn't happy.

"I don't have time," Kung Fo said in Chinese, "my friend needs me, I'll be back later with double what I owe you."

"You better fucking had be," Tsang Su replied, also in Chinese, "or it'll be you and your mother's head on a pike for all in New London to see."

Kung Fo made a minute spitting sound and climbed into his pod. Was Tsang Su serious this time? Or was it one of his many empty threats? Kung Fo decided he didn't care as he took off and headed for Von Croft Tower.

15

Ricky hung up. He didn't know if he was going to make it to the roof, let alone escape in Kung Fo's pod, but he had to try. Von Croft couldn't get away with what he'd done. Next to the camera phone booth, conveniently, was a service elevator. Ricky walked in and pressed the button for the top floor. During the ride up, he thought about Deanna. How could she have betrayed him like that? He thought he loved her, she thought he loved her, and she used that. He hoped Kung Fo was on his way soon. He didn't want to be stuck here. Not with the elite squad patrolling the building. But Ricky felt safe in the elevator. Safe in the knowledge he was bypassing them with each floor.

The elevator door opened with a dull, almost spotlike, tone and Ricky thought of the antique movie about a man stuck in a skyscraper with a group of terrorists. He exited the elevator and was greeted by a gold encrusted room. It glittered in its opulence. The only light, coming from lamps in alcoves built into the wall. Ricky wondered if all the floors were like this, but knowing men like Adam Von Croft, this probably wasn't the case. Across from him, was a grandiose door with Von Croft's name written in a signature style. He'd seen this door many times on his visits with Deanna, but it never failed to disgust him. How can Von Croft live in such luxury, when below people suffered in squalor? He unholstered his pistol and it scanned the floor. Its barrel opened up, the silencer came out and the barrel closed again, like a clockwork toy from the ancient times. He walked to the door and opened it, sure that he'd never leave through it.

The apartment was spacious and, again, lit by lamps in alcoves in the walls. It was night time now, and the rain fell in buckets against the large, floor to ceiling, window. Von Croft was stood with his back to Ricky, behind a desk made of oak and finished with the finest resin, looking out at New London.

"I knew," he began, as Ricky came forward, gun at the ready, "that it was only a matter of time before you came to kill me, Ricky," he turns to face him and smiles, his veneers gleaming with anticipation, "but you see," he clicks his fingers and four men and two drones arrive, "that is quite impossible."

Diving for cover, Ricky opened fire. The drones

following him and firing bullets of their own, one caught Ricky in the calf. Von Croft and the four men dove for cover also. Ricky opened fire on the two drones and dispatched them almost instantly. He was amazed at how powerful this pistol was. The four men opened fire and a fire fight ensued until all four of them clicked empty. Ricky took his chance and shot the four minions. Blood on the lavish walls, the lamps glowed red with gore and Ricky limped over to where Von Croft hid.

"Please," Von Croft stammered. He had a real look of actual fear in his grey eyes. Ricky felt no pity and aimed at his face.

Suddenly to his right, he heard the dull tone of the elevator opening, and the smile on Von Croft's face returned. Outside the window, Ricky spotted Kung Fo's pod nearing the building and starting to lift upwards. He looked back at Von Croft and fired. The blood spoiled Von Croft's suit and Ricky was glad. He limped over to a bookcase and took cover. Above him, Ricky noticed an air vent, so he climbed the bookcase to gain access to a better hiding place. The pain in his calf made it difficult to climb but he did it anyway. He climbed into the vent just as six more men arrived with smart rifles. The big guy who'd given him the revolver a few weeks ago at the high rise quarter, walked round the table to see Von Croft dead. He ordered the other men to leave the room, Ricky had himself propped over the vent opening, if his legs gave way he'd fall and get shot probably.

"I know your still here Walters," the big guy called, "you'd better come out and face me like a man."

Ricky dropped from the vent and onto the big guy's shoulders, firing his gun at random places, hoping to get a good shot but also hoping to stay on his shoulders. The big guy moved so erratically that Ricky fell off and onto the floor. The big guy picks him up and throws him out the window. Ricky free fell for a few seconds, wondering if he was going to die tonight. But just as he was about to hit the concrete outside, Kung Fo arrived and he landed on the roof of the pod, nearly shattering it.

"Holy shit!" Kung Fo shouted as he got out, "you ok?"

"Felt worse," Ricky answered, and climbed into the passenger seat.

Kung Fo then took off.

"You no look too hot misser Walters," Kung Fo said, "we get you some water and some product and we fix you up in no time."

"Thanks," Ricky said wearily, "I need to party after that."

"You cover in blood, Ricky," Kung Fo said, in shock.

"Not mine," Ricky replied, "Von Croft's."

"You stomp on him too?"

"No,"

"Why there blood on leg?

"I got shot by those damn drones," Ricky said, and fell asleep.

They got to his mother's shop in no time at all. Ricky started looking white as they landed, so Kung Fo radioed his mother to come up and help. Tsang Su was still there too, but Kung Fo didn't have time to be doing business, he had his best customer to save. Tsang Su saw the gravity of the situation and helped them bring Ricky inside.

"It's not safe for him here," they pleaded with him in Chinese, "that elite squad will know where he is in no time."

"Well we better fix him up quick then," he replied, irritably in Chinese.

A day later, Ricky woke up. He was greeted with a brown ceiling with a silver, metallic ceiling fan. Turning, turning. He sat up and wiped his eyes. He winced as he tried to move his leg and remembered he'd been shot. Frustrated, he tried to stand, and fell right on his face. His cheek felt nice on the cool tiling. He stood up again, hands suddenly appeared and helped him back into bed. It was Kung Fo's mother. She said something in Chinese.

“She say you should stay in bed,” a voice behind her said, it was Kung Fo himself, “leg need to heal,” he drew out the word ‘heal’ just to fit the stereotype.

“How long was I out?” Ricky asked.

“Twenty four hour,” Kung Fo said.

“I killed Von Croft,” Ricky said.

“You no worry about him no more,” Kung Fo said, “we’ve all been talking, and we going to help you, they come here guns blazing, so do we.”

“Thanks guys,” Ricky said, and fell back to sleep.

16

A few hours later, he woke again and heard voices coming from a distance. He sat up and looked around. He was in a small room, looked like a store room. He then realised he was in the back room of Kung Fo's mother's shop. He was laying on a faded white, leather sofa. His leg still stinging a bit from where he got shot. He tried to stand, but couldn't, so he resigned to just sitting on the sofa.

"Ah, you awake," Kung Fo came in from the shop floor.

"Yeah," Ricky replied, "but I'm fucking gerning something awful."

Kung Fo smiled and handed Ricky a small vial of Ko Sang, a syringe and a spoon. Ricky looked around for a lighter, found one, and proceeded to cook and took a hit there on the sofa. The Ko Sang felt great coursing through his veins, almost orgasmic. He sat back and let the high wash over him.

Once he could function, and the pain in his leg

had slightly subsided, Ricky decided to get up. He walked to the front to be greeted by a group of people. Kung Fo was one of them. Kung Fo then proceeded to introduce Ricky to all of them. Tsang Su, Chang Hua, Tsang Su's little brother Tsang Ping, and Kung Fo's mother Kung Mae. Ricky shook hands with all of them then turned to Kung Fo.

"Is this all we've got?"

"Best we do on short notice, main man Ricky."

"What guns can we get?"

"We have this," Kung Fo lifted Ricky's smart pistol and everyone gasped in awe, "and Tsang Su said he knows Triad people, but he lies a lot, so," Kung Fo shrugged.

"We need a plan of action then," Ricky said.

The rain beat down hard on New Chinatown that night. Ricky, and the group of people he'd just that day met, waited outside the shop for the elite squad to show up. Tsang Ping paced across the street and back again several times before Tsang Su told him to stop. Ricky felt for his pistol in his pocket. It felt good knowing it was there but, without the others holding, they were screwed. Chang Hua took a phone call, then left and came back again a few minutes later with several sports bags and a huge smile on his face. He said something in Chinese and the others gathered round him, chatting excitedly. Kung Fo then lifted a shotgun to inspect it and Ricky walked over, curious at all the commotion. In the bags were several guns and ammunition. Ricky felt a little relieved but he'd seen the hardware the elite squad were packing before, and how good they were at using them, so he had his doubts. But maybe Kung Fo and the gang could surprise him. Maybe they could pull it out of the proverbial bag. It was moot to worry, as New Chinatown was full of extended families, everyone usually looked after each other, someone had to have their backs if shit got ugly.

A few hours into the vigil, a small fleet of armored pods landed outside the shop and, aiming at the small ragtag group of people, the elite squad piled out. There was a standoff as everybody aimed at everyone else. Even Kung Mae aimed a shotgun, this little old lady aiming this big gun, it was almost comical.

"Give up the junkie," the leader said, "and we'll leave you alone."

The ragtags cocked their weapons, and the squad did also.

"I'll handle this," said a voice from the back, it was the big guy.

"Ricky, Ricky, Ricky," he said, "what are we going to do?"

The smart pistol throbbed in Ricky's hand,

it was scanning the area and its barrel, like a mechanical toy, became larger. The bullet count increased and a stock came out the back. Ricky went from holding it like a pistol, to holding it like a rifle. A flash of lightning and a rumble of thunder made Ricky look up to see a silent chopper hovering over their location.

Ricky thought that, with Von Croft dead, that the elite squad would be disbanded. He was wrong. A son that Ricky never knew Von Croft had, had taken over from his father and ordered him dead. Sniveling little college drop out probably, but then again, with daddy's money he probably got the best education in New London.

So here they were, standing in the pouring rain, pointing guns at each other.

"Paton Von Croft wants you dead," the big guy said, "and we always deliver. So just hand over the junkie fuck, and the rest of you don't die today."

Everyone stood their ground and the big guy laughed.

"Ok," he said, turning to go back to his pod, "fire at will guys."

A fire fight ensued in the middle of the street and everyone ran for cover.

It was when Ricky stopped firing, he realised Tsang Ping hadn't made it. When Tsang Su realised, he went ballistic. Firing, he ran out and took one of them down, before getting shot in the head himself. His blood and brains flowing down into the sewer. The red river connecting with that of his brother's. Chang Hua, Kung Fo and Kung Mae hid behind some crates, Ricky behind a vintage Ford Fiesta car. When the squad clicked empty momentarily, Ricky took his chance to join them, firing as he ran across the street, to where the others were.

"There goes our Triad contact," Ricky said.

"I tell you," Kung Fo said, "he lie, a lot!"

Ricky looked above the crates and gunfire forced him to duck for cover.

Suddenly, they heard one of the squad say "smoke 'em out!" and the chopper shone a searchlight at them and opened fire. They ran as fast as they could in different directions.

"Spread out," the big guy said, "they can't be far."

Chang Hua hid inside a shop, in the fitting room. The guard who followed him was female, although she didn't look it. Out of the slit in the curtain, Chang Hua noticed her searching through the clothes racks for him. He made a call to the guy who called him before.

"We didn't make it," he said in Chinese "Tsang Su and Tsang Ping are dead."

"Try to stay where you are," the voice, also in Chinese, said, "we'll be at your location in five minutes."

Just as he hung up, the curtain was ripped down and the woman-thing aimed at him. Before she could get a shot, Chang Hua grabbed the curtain rail with one hand and the barrel of her rifle in the other, and, moving the aim off him, bashed her skull several times until she fell to the floor, dead.

Kung Fo hid in a restaurant, in the kitchen. His pursuer was a black man with ever shine tattoos glowing all over his face. Kung Fo ducked behind the service counter before he got spotted, the chef calmly asking him in Chinese what he was doing.

"The guy out there," Kung Fo replied in Chinese, "he's just killed my friends and now he's after me. Try to act natural."

The chef did so as the squad man came up to the service counter.

"Where is he?"

The chef shook his head.

"No English," he said, and the guard sighed in exasperation.

Kung Fo took his opportunity and jumped up and fired, killing the squadman instantly.

Kung Mae was hiding in her shop, behind the counter, her shotgun empty. She looked desperately for another weapon but found only a meat cleaver. The guard came in, he was hyspanic and large.

Almost as big as the big guy who wanted Kung Fo's friend Ricky dead. She wouldn't let that happen. She thought back to her childhood, when she was living on the surface with her mother, being taught how to chop chicken with a cleaver. The guard came by the counter and Kung Mae took her chance. She jumped up and swooped the cleaver down and into the guard's skull. There was a shot and Kung Mae and the guard were dead.

Ricky ran down an alleyway. His pursuer quickly on his tail. He was Afro-Carribean and quite fast. He came to a dead end in the alleyway and turned to face the man chasing him. Ricky smiled, and the Afro-Carribean man smiled back. They both aimed, wondering who would fire first. The matched beads of sweat and rain ran down their foreheads. Their fingers twitching over the triggers. The alleyway lit only by the neon lights of the street beyond. The Afro-Carribean pulled the trigger and Ricky started. Empty.

"Shit!" he shouted, and Ricky laughed as he pulled the trigger, shooting the man dead.

17

Kung Fo, Chang Hua and Ricky emerged onto the street again. There was only the big guy left now and Ricky felt it was personal. But when they got there, the big guy wasn't at all nervous. He pointed to the sky. The chopper. They'd forgotten the chopper looming over them. Then he clicked his fingers and more men from the elite squad arrived. They were surrounded. Nowhere to run. Up shit creek without a paddle, some would say. Suddenly, there was a huge explosion, and the chopper fell in a ball of flame. Gunfire from all directions. Then a fleet of more armored pods landed. The cavalry had arrived, it seemed. What seemed like the entire Triad family poured out, guns blazing. Ricky and the others took shelter in Kung Mae's shop. It was there Kung Fo discovered his mother, dead in a red pool behind the counter. Shot through the heart by an elite squad man with a meat cleaver in his head. Kung Fo remembered the time when he fell and scraped his knee in the street. His mother came running out and smothered him in kisses to prevent him from crying. She wasn't here now, and the tears flowed freely down his cheeks. Ricky put his hand on Kung Fo's shoulder for comfort. He felt guilty that he'd brought this on Kung Fo's doorstep. Kung Mae would still be alive if Ricky had just given himself up. His damn pride.

Outside, the gunfire had stopped. They all went out to investigate, a little tentative as to who actually won the gunfight. Bodies lay everywhere in the street, the big guy among them. They were then greeted by a short man in a white suit. He spoke to Chang Hua in Chinese, who then told

Kung Fo, who then translated into broken English.

"He say they will avenge the fallen."

"Ok, what about me?"

"He say they give you money to start new life, but to never return to New Chinatown, you are like disease, and brought many death to this place."

Ricky understood what was going on here, and thought better of speaking out. The short man handed Ricky a briefcase from one of the pods. Ricky opened it to find thirty thousand credits inside.

PART 4:

Epilogue

17

A few days later, Kung Fo was helping Ricky pack his things. He still couldn't believe Ricky decided to start a new life in the outer orbit holiday resort. But, that was Ricky, always thinking big. Ricky picked up his gun, they weren't going to let him have that where he was going.

"Here," he offered it to Kung Fo, "I want you to have this, it's the least I can do."

"Thank," Kung Fo replied.

They gathered the rest of his things and left for the roof. Kung Fo half expected to see Tsang Su waiting for him next to his pod, but he wasn't. It made him feel empty inside. They got in and took off.

Flying over New London for the last time, Ricky remembered how eager he was to be the big boss, the big cheese, but now he was happy to see the back of the place. He had a scheduled flight from Neo-Heathrow to the outer orbit on an orbital six twenty super pod, they were bigger than bus pods,

Ricky had heard. He was eager to taste the food, he hadn't eaten in a long time. Ko Sang just about eradicates your appetite, and Ricky had been on the stuff for a while now. But now it was wearing off, he felt a real hunger for a nice big beef burger. Ready made or cooked to perfection, he didn't care, he was jonesing for one right there and then.

"Can we stop someplace before we hit the pod port?"

"Where you wan' go?"

"Anywhere that I can get a beef burger."

They stopped at a floating diner and got a take out. The burger was nice and greasy. The fries, salty and crisp. 'Absolute perfection' he thought, as he bit into the burger and felt the grease explode in his mouth.

They got to Neo-Heathrow after they finished their meal. They said their goodbyes and Ricky boarded. They never saw each other again. As he was seated, Ricky checked his bag. Kung Fo had said something, as they were chowing down on the burgers and fries, about a nice surprise in his overnight bag, he looked and saw it was a nice big block of Ko Sang.

"Nothing like nice high in zero gravity" he'd said, and Ricky believed him.

Sat across from him was a woman he thought he knew, matter of fact he KNEW he knew her. It was

Lisa, the Supreme Colony Boss.

She looked over and noticed he was staring at her. She smiled shyly and bit her bottom lip.

'How the fuck did she get out this time?' he thought.

THE END

www.ingramcontent.com/pod-product-compliance
Lightning Source LLC
LaVergne TN
LVHW010106110826
845155LV00028B/515